Spectacularly
Beautiful

STORY BY
Lisa Lucas

PICTURES BY
Laurie Stein

Brooklyn, NY

Every day,
Shahad came to school
with perfect hair.

It was perfectly combed
and perfectly braided
and the ribbons...they were perfectly tied.

One day, Ms. Truong set up tables with paper and pencils and pots of paint.

"I want you to draw a memory.
But not any memory.
This one has to come
from the place you were born."

Trivien drew
a shiny red bicyle.

Tuyet painted
a big bowl of rice.

Tierney drew
a bunch of kids
running through tall,
green grass.

And Shahad
just sat there...

doing nothing.

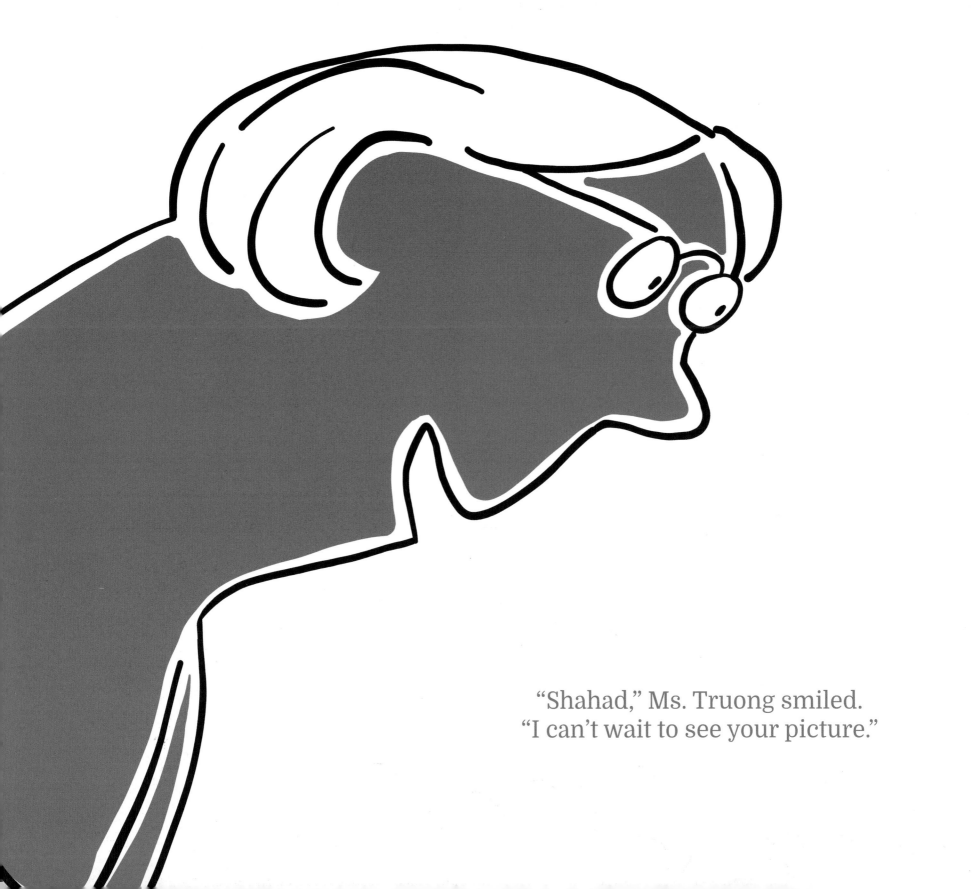

"Shahad," Ms. Truong smiled.
"I can't wait to see your picture."

So Shahad
quickly scribbled
a pile of
broken bricks
and crabby
looking faces.

Ms. Truong asked the children to sit on the carpet so they could share their pictures with one another.

Tuyet
held hers up first.

"In my country, my Grandma
made me eat rice.
There it was every single day...
a big bowl full of white,
sticky goo...ICK!"

Then Tierney held up
his picture really high.

"I loved running
in the grass...

round and round and round
with my friends until
we dropped to the ground laughing."

Trivien pointed to
the bicycle in his picture.

"In my country,
everyone rode bikes. *Everyone!*
Just before I had to leave,
my uncle gave me
this brand new, red bicycle.

It was perfect.
But I had to leave it behind."

Trivien
looked down,
his eyes growing wet.
Ms. Truong
leaned toward him.

"You know,
there is a used bike store
just around the corner
from the school.
I don't know if they have
a red one, but maybe you
and your parents
could stop in and
have a look someday."

Shahad stood up.
"In my country,
we have the best food
in the whole world.
Our hummus
is my favorite.
It's not as good here."

Then, Shahad
looked around
at her friends,
and their bright,
happy drawings
and pointed
to her own.

"But these
are the bricks
that made
my eye look like this...
and my leg...like this."

Then, the children took their seats
and Shahad quickly plopped herself down.

The bell rang
and the children
handed their pictures
to Ms. Truong.
She stopped Shahad
on the way out
and told her how much
she liked the braids
in her hair.

Shahad smiled...a little.

The next morning, Ms. Truong told Shahad
how much she liked the yellow ribbons in her hair.
Shahad smiled...a bit more.

And just before lunch,
Shahad marched up to Ms. Truong and asked,
"Do you think I'm beautiful?"

Ms. Truong looked at Shahad,
paused and smiled,
"I think you are spectacularly beautiful."

Day after day,
Shahad asked
the same
question.

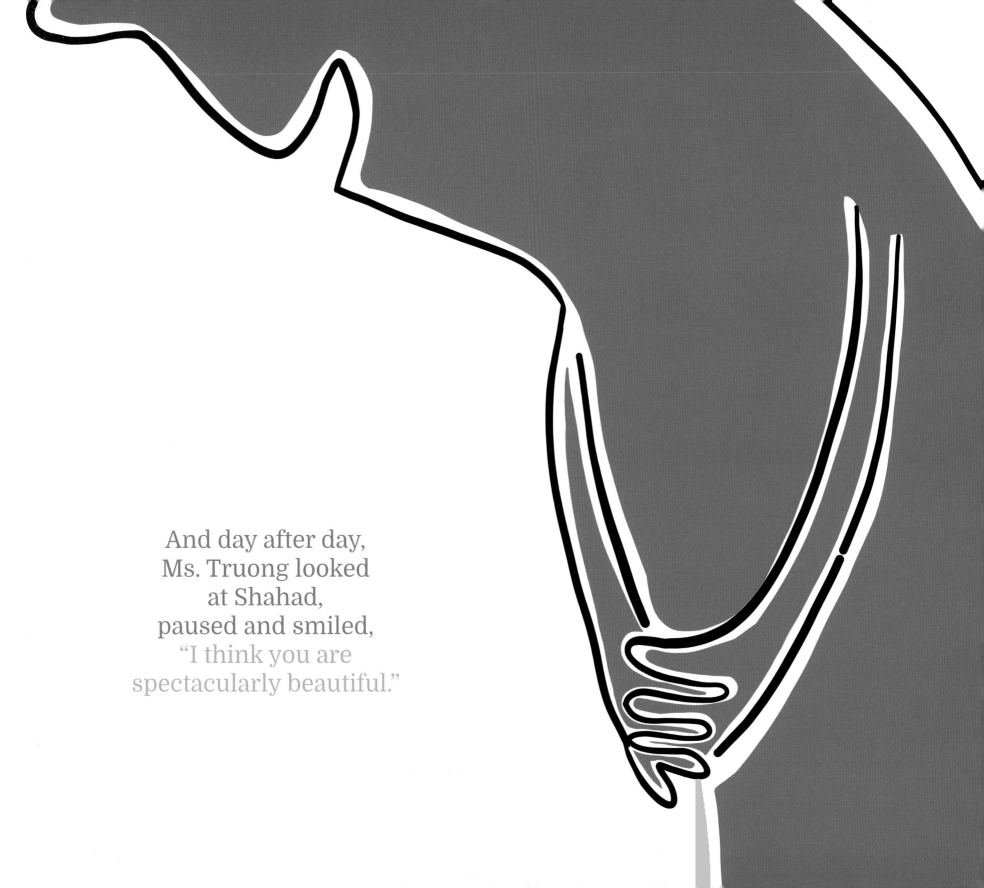

And day after day,
Ms. Truong looked
at Shahad,
paused and smiled,
"I think you are
spectacularly beautiful."

Then the last day of school arrived.

Ms. Truong looked a little sad.

"I'm going to miss you
over the summer.
But I will be teaching
children your age in a country
that has a few problems.

And those children...
they'll remind me of you."

Days went by.

The summer ended.

The first
day of school
arrived.

Ms. Truong welcomed
the new children to her class.

They all had a great first day.

When the bell rang at the end of the day,
Ms. Truong led the children out.
On the way, she spotted Shahad.
They looked at each other for a long time.

Then, Ms. Truong
showed Shahad her scar.
It was new.
"Do you think I'm beautiful?"

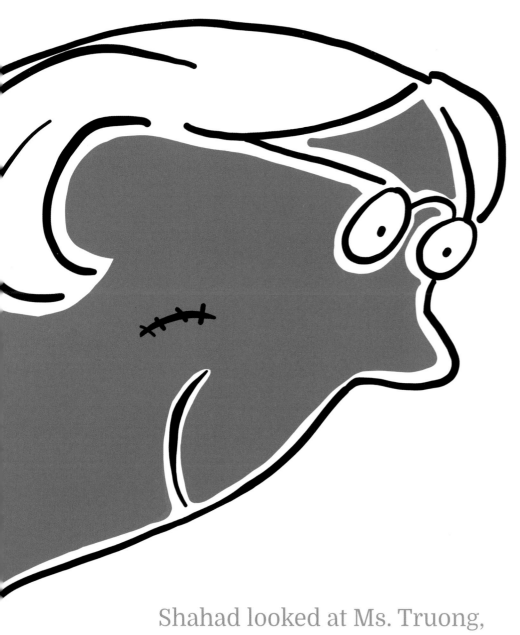

Shahad looked at Ms. Truong,
paused and smiled,
"I think you are
spectacularly beautiful."

AUTHOR'S NOTE:

I've worked in high-needs schools in Toronto, Canada for many years. I've taught kids who have challenges that would bring many adults down. And I marvel at their resilience and grit. They don't crumble. They don't fall. They move forward...sometimes a little more slowly, but forward is forward. Shahad was one of those students. And though the injuries inflicted on her were far more serious than those depicted in this book, her feisty self-confidence, and forward-thinking inspired me to write this book. She really is Spectacularly Beautiful.

www.lisalucas.ca

Spectacularly Beautiful

Text © 2018 by Lisa Lucas
Illustrations © 2018 by Laurie Stein

Published by POW!
a division of powerHouse Packaging & Supply, Inc.
32 Adams Street, Brooklyn, NY 11201-1021
info@powkidsbooks.com • www.powkidsbooks.com
www.powerHouseBooks.com
www.powerHousePackaging.com

Printed by TWP

Library of Congress Control Number: 2018938400

ISBN: 978-1-57687-891-0

10 9 8 7 6 5 4 3 2 1

Printed in **Malaysia**